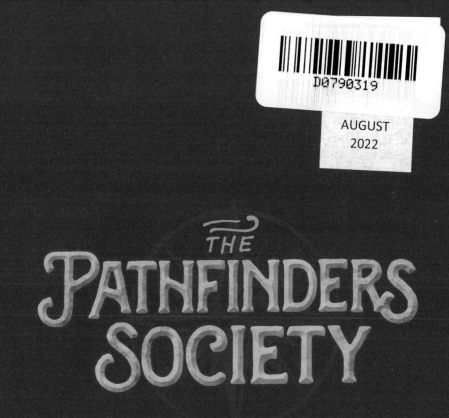

THE PATHFINDERS SOCIETY

The Path So Far

AS THEIR ADVENTURE CONTINUES, Kyle, Vic, Beth, Harry, and Nate follow the path left by Henry Merriweather to discover a mysterious new world below Windrose.

With their motto "Plus Ultra!" (More Beyond!) leading them, their trail turns and twists through creepy caverns and terrifying tests, until the path suddenly ends at Fairly's Quarry. The friends suspect that the Fairlys don't share Henry's vision of Windrose and are hatching a decades-old plot that may destroy the town.

A quick, magical trip to the Historical Society proves their hunch is right. They see the moment the vow between Henry and his brother Jacob was broken, with Jacob selling his share of the town to the Fairlys.

But time is of the essence to save Camp Pathfinder and Merriweather Castle. Henry's great-niece Mildred is being forced to sell his half to the Fairlys!

The kids must forge their own path past the tricky Labyrinth and underground to find the Crystal Cavern, only to face the legendary and deadly Creeper!

But the cavern floods, and the friends barely escape with their lives. They soon find themselves washed up back at what seems to be Camp Pathfinder, only to meet a familiar but mysteriously young friend . . . *Plus Ultra!*

Meet the Pathfinders

KYLE is the new kid in town. He's always got a sketchbook in his pocket—and drawing is a very useful tool when you're connecting the dots on a treasure hunt!

BETH is super-organized and a bit of a history nerd. Need to go forward following a map? Or backward in time to solve a mystery? She's your girl.

HARRY is a goofball whose mouth sometimes moves faster than his brain. But his love of magic means he spots what's hidden in a tricky situation.

VICTORIA (VIC) is a popular cheerleader—and a secret math whiz. She figures out numbers and patterns along the path before anybody else even sees them.

NATE likes to invent stuff. His motto? *A.B.R.: Always Be Ready*. He's the guy you want on your team when you need solutions . . . *fast*!

THE PATHFINDERS SOCIETY

The Legend of the Lost Boy

Francesco Sedita &
Prescott Seraydarian
illustrated by
Steve Hamaker

VIKING

VIKING
An imprint of Penguin Random House LLC, New York

First published in the United States of America by Viking,
an imprint of Penguin Random House LLC, 2022

Visit us online at penguinrandomhouse.com.

Library of Congress Cataloging-in-Publication Data is available.

Manufactured in China

ISBN 9780593206195 (hardcover)
ISBN 9780593206201 (paperback)

1 3 5 7 9 10 8 6 4 2

TOPL

Book design by Steve Hamaker and Jim Hoover

Dedications

This book is dedicated to my lifetime friend, dreamer, and fellow Pathfinder, Prescott. People, if we only knew then what we do now, when you were wearing a white button-down and a vest, in Third North. —FS

To Francesco, for his profound patience and partnership. —PS

For my cousin Eric Smith. Thank you for helping me color these last two books! You have inspired and encouraged me as an artist our entire lives. —SH

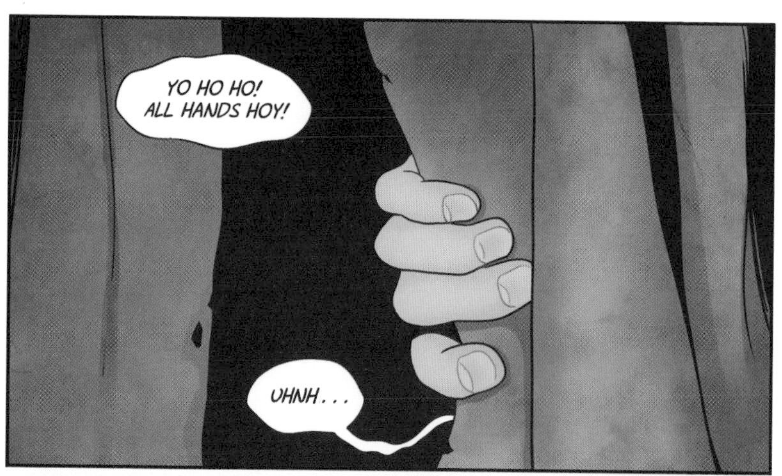

DING! DING!

THERE! THERE!

WHERE AM I?

LOOK YONDER! WE FOUND IT. THE PATH IS AHEAD!

CAPTAIN!

AHA! LOOKS LIKE THIS LOST BOY HAS FOUND ITS WAY, AYE, LADS?

MAKE FAST . . .

PLUS ULTRA!
ONWARD!

KEEP TRUE, LADS.

THERE ARE MONSTERS GUARDING THESE WATERS. SCYLLA AND CHARYBDIS!

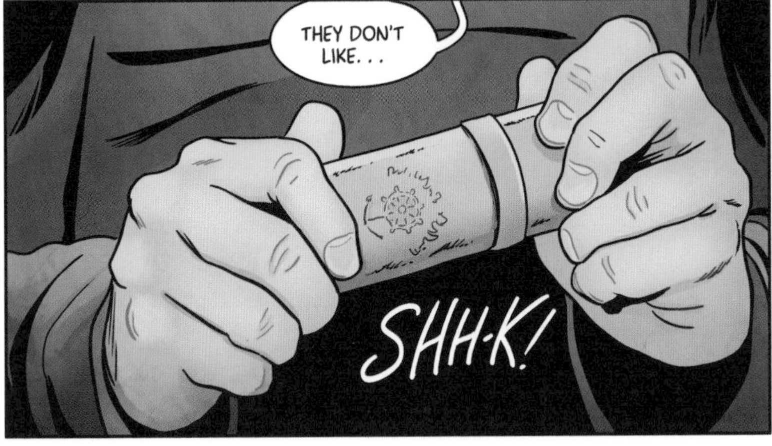
THEY DON'T LIKE. . .
SHH-K!

. . .TRESPASSERS!
CRRR
CHI-
CHI...

CAP'N!
CRASH!!

THE OTHER IS HERE!
THEY'S GOT US!
CRASH!

MAKE HASTE!

THE PATH IS FADING.

THE PATH
IS FADING!

DO YOU HEAR?

YES, I HEAR.

I HEAR . . .

I . . .
HEAR . . .
NATE!
WHAT DID
YOU HEAR?

Chapter ONE

GOOD MORNING, SUNSHINE.

VIC?

THAT'S RIGHT, IT'S ME. WHAT PATH IS FADING?

WHAT'S GOING ON? WHERE ARE WE?
THE "*WHERE*" IS EASY. WE'RE BACK AT CAMP PATHFINDER. IT'S THE "*WHEN*" THAT'S WEIRD.

YOU'VE BEEN OUT OF IT SINCE WE GOT HERE.
CLICK!
FLASH!
SOMETHING HAPPENED TO ME WHEN I TOUCHED REGGIE . . . WHILE WE WERE ON THE SPIDER.

WAIT!
WHERE'S REGGIE?!
I'M SO SORRY, NATE. BUT REGGIE'S GONE.

WHAT HAPPENED?
WE BARELY ESCAPED THE CAVERNS!
YOU REALLY DON'T REMEMBER?
ONE OF FARLEY'S DRILLS BROKE THROUGH AND CAUSED A FLOOD!
WE RODE THAT CRAZY ROBOT-SPIDER AND SAW A CRACK IN THE GROUND. WINDROSE IS IN DANGER!

WE CRASHED INTO A TREE AND THAT'S WHEN REGGIE SLIPPED OUT OF YOUR HANDS.
WHEN WE WERE UNDERWATER SOMETHING HAPPENED TO US. WE ENDED UP BACK HERE, BUT MILDRED WAS--
MILDRED
SHE'S OUR AGE! I SORTA REMEMBER THAT PART.

OKAY, I TOLD YOU, NOW YOU TELL ME. WHAT DID YOU HEAR? WHAT DOES "THE PATH IS FADING" MEAN? YOU WERE MUMBLING IN YOUR SLEEP.
I THINK IT MEANS THAT WE'RE CLOSE TO FIGURING THIS OUT, BUT WE'RE RUNNING OUT OF TIME.

I'M WORRIED ABOUT YOU. IT SEEMS LIKE YOU'RE WORSE TODAY.
I'M NOT. IT'S FINE.
I THINK WE SHOULD TELL THE OTHERS.

NO! WE CAN'T! AT LEAST NOT YET. LOOK, I NEED TO TELL YOU SOMETHING. . .
WHAT?

THIS IS JUST FOR YOU, OKAY?
OKAY?
I'M SERIOUS!
I SAID OKAY!

WE'RE ON THE RIGHT PATH. I THINK WE'RE CLOSE.

WHAT'S WRONG?
I THINK SOMETHING IS GOING TO HAPPEN THAT WILL LEAD US TO THE END.

WHAT IS AT THE END?
THE TREASURE?

HOW DO YOU KNOW ALL OF THIS?

I JUST DO!
AND WHEN THE TIME COMES, SO WILL YOU. BUT LET'S NOT TELL EVERYONE ELSE YET. AT LEAST NOT UNTIL IT HAPPENS.

PROMISE YOU WON'T SAY ANYTHING. VOW?
I DON'T KNOW WHAT I'M PROMISING!

I PROMISE IT WILL BE OKAY, IF YOU PROMISE NOT TO SAY ANYTHING.
AAAARRRRGH, FINE. OKAY.
VOW!

YES, ALRIGHT ALREADY. I VOW!
NATE, GOOD MORNING, OLD PAL!

NATE'S AWAKE!
YOU OKAY, NATE? YOU LOOK A LITTLE OFF.

NAAAATE. BUDDY? CAN YOU HEAR ME?
WELL, I CAN SMELL YOU.
SEE? HE'S FINE.

WHAT DID YOU ALL FIND OUT?
WELL, WE'RE DEFINITELY IN 1962.
AND THERE'S ANOTHER MOON FESTIVAL.

IT'S LIKE WE'RE IN A HISTORY BOOK. BUT FOR REAL.
YEAH, LOVE IT. NO PHONES, NO INTERNET. YAY.

DOES ANY OF THE WEIRD TIME-SHIFTING MAKE SENSE TO ANYONE ELSE?
NOT REALLY.
THIS SHIFT WAS DEFINITELY MORE INTENSE.

KYLE, CAN I SEE YOUR NOTEBOOK?
SURE.

Robot head
Reggie?
tracks make a pattern.
Possible Maze?
I THINK THERE'S AN ENERGY UNDER WINDROSE. WE SAW IT IN THE CAVERN BEFORE IT FLOODED!

FIRST THERE WERE TIME SLIPS WHERE WE COULD SEE OTHER TIMES.
BUT NOW WE'RE NOT JUST SEEING THE PAST . . . WE'RE IN IT!
HOW DO YOU KNOW ALL OF THIS?
I JUST DO.

YOU'RE UNUSUALLY QUIET, VIC. WHAT DO YOU THINK?
I THINK WE HAVE TO FIGURE OUT WHY WE'RE HERE. IT HAS TO BE CONNECTED TO WHAT JACOB SAID IN THE CAVERN.

AND FIND THE TREASURE?
WE HAVE TO FIGURE THIS OUT. WE NEED MILDRED.

MILDRED MERRI-WEATHER. AT YOUR SERVICE!
MILDRED
UHHH, WHAT DO YOU HAVE THERE?

I WAS ABLE TO GET CAMP UNIFORMS FOR ALL OF YOU! I FEEL LIKE THERE'S A REASON I FOUND YOU ALL!
MORE THAN YOU KNOW.

SO, YOU SAID YOU'RE EXCHANGE CAMPERS FROM CAMP--
UH . . . WHATSITCALLED.
CAMP WHATSITCALLED? I'VE NEVER HEARD OF--

IT'S A NEW PROGRAM, AND WE DON'T WANT TO DRAW TOO MUCH ATTENTION.
IF YOU DON'T WANT TO STICK OUT, PUT THESE ON.

COOOOL!
THEY LOOK SO OLD-SCHOOL.
THEY'RE NOT FOR SCHOOL, AND THEY'RE BRAND-NEW THIS SEASON . . .

DON'T MIND HIM. THEY'RE CLEAN, SO THEY'RE PERFECT! THANK YOU!
sniff.

WHAT'S IN THERE?
IT'S HIS BAG OF TRICKS.
A.B.R.

ALWAYS BE READY!
MILDRED

HOW DO WE LOOK?
VERY RETRO.
I LIKE YOUR NECKERCHIEF!
THANKS.

I WASN'T SURE AT FIRST, BUT I HAVE TO ADMIT, THIS IS PRETTY CUTE AS FAR AS UNIFORMS GO.
VIC LOVES A UNIFORM.

WHAT UNIFORM DO YOU NORMALLY WEAR?
OH, I WAS A-- I AM A CHEERLEADER.

YOU SHOULD TRY IT, IT'S FUN.
I'M DEFINITELY NOT CHEERLEADER MATERIAL.
WELL, IT'S NOT AS MUCH FUN AS BEING A PATHFINDER.
MILDRED

YES, WE GOT HER!
VIC IS ONE OF US!
FROM AN A TO . . . WHAT ARE WE? C'S?
WHAT? NOT AT ALL! WE ARE A+! LOOK AT US! WHO ELSE DO YOU KNOW THAT IS ACTUALLY ON A TREASURE HUNT?

ALL PATHFINDERS PLEASE REPORT TO THE MESS HALL.

SPEAKING OF ALWAYS BEING READY! GET DRESSED AND LET'S HEAD OUT.

MOON F
YOU'VE PICKED A REALLY GOOD TIME TO VISIT. IT'S THE SUPER MOON FESTIVAL! THIS YEAR IS A SPECIAL ONE. IT ONLY HAPPENS--

ONCE IN A BLUE MOON?
HA HA! SOMETHING LIKE THAT.

WHOA. CAN YOU SAY DÉJà VU?
I CAN SAY IT. BUT DON'T ASK ME WHAT IT MEANS.

IS SOMETHING WRONG? ARE YOU OKAY?

OH, SURE! EVERYTHING'S FINE! JUST ANOTHER DAY AT CAMP . . . IN *1962*. NOTHING WEIRD HERE AT ALL.

LOOK OUT, FELLAS, OR YOU MIGHT GET STRUCK BY LIGHTNING!
FRY GAL!
MAYBE IT RUNS IN THE FAMILY!

IGNORE THE *GOON PLATOON.*

I GUESS JERKS HAVE BEEN AROUND FOR A LONG, LONG TIME.
LEAVE HER ALONE.

WHO'S GONNA MAKE US?

SHOVE!

JONAS FAIRLY, THAT'S ENOUGH.

FAIRLY?

YOUR FAMILY HAS ALWAYS BEEN TROUBLE.
COME WITH ME.

WHAT JERKS!
I CAN'T STAND BULLIES.

DON'T WORRY ABOUT THEM, I'M USED TO IT. THERE ARE LOTS OF PEOPLE IN WINDROSE WHO DON'T LIKE MY FAMILY.

WELCOME, PATHFINDERS, TO THE SUMMER OF 1962!

IT'S OUR ANNIVERSARY, AND WE HAVE SOME FUN ACTIVITIES PLANNED, WITH THE SUPER MOON FESTIVAL AND A TIME CAPSULE CEREMONY AT THE END OF THE SEASON.

AS YOU KNOW, THIS CAMP WAS FOUNDED BY HENRY MERRIWEATHER--
FRY GUY!

HA! HA! HA! HA
HA! HA!
MILDRED

HA! HA
HA!
HA! HA!
ALL RIGHT, SETTLE DOWN. THAT'S ENOUGH.

WE HAVE A NEW MOVIE ABOUT CAMP THAT I THINK YOU WILL ENJOY VERY MUCH.

NOT THIS AGAIN.
WHAT DO YOU MEAN, *AGAIN?*
NOTHING, NOTHING!

BONK!

OW! STOP, I'M DELICATE!

BE SURE TO PAY ATTENTION. I HEAR THERE ARE CLUES FOR THE TREASURE HUNT . . .
THE TREASURE THAT WE WILL NEVER FIND . . .
SHH!!

CAMP PATHFINDER: EVERY PATH MUST BE FOLLOWED!
CAMP
PATHFINDER

CAMP PATHFINDER IS FOR THE CURIOUS. FOR COUNTLESS GENERATIONS . . .

. . . PEOPLE HAVE SET OUT TO EXPLORE THE WORLD.

PATHFINDERS FIND THE PATH-- NO MATTER HOW AND NO MATTER WHERE.

PREPARATION IS THE PATHFINDER'S BEST TOOL.
A.B.R.!

ACROSS THE LAND . . .

THROUGH THE WATERS, ALWAYS BRAVELY VENTURING INTO THE UNKNOWN.

SEARCHING FOR TREASURES AT HOME AND ABROAD.
THAT'S THE--
LOST BOY!

HOW DO YOU KNOW THAT?
OW!
LUCKY GUESS?

DO YOU KNOW ANYTHING ABOUT THAT SHIP, MILDRED?

NOT REALLY, BUT MY UNCLES ALWAYS TALKED ABOUT IT.

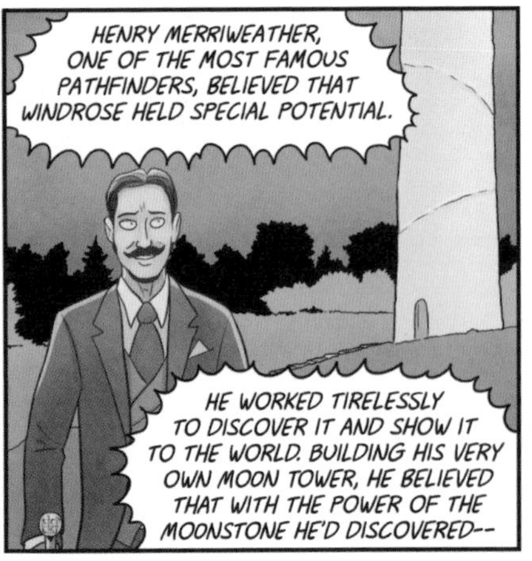
HENRY MERRIWEATHER, ONE OF THE MOST FAMOUS PATHFINDERS, BELIEVED THAT WINDROSE HELD SPECIAL POTENTIAL.
HE WORKED TIRELESSLY TO DISCOVER IT AND SHOW IT TO THE WORLD. BUILDING HIS VERY OWN MOON TOWER, HE BELIEVED THAT WITH THE POWER OF THE MOONSTONE HE'D DISCOVERED--

DON'T FRY!
HA HA!
HA HA!
HA HA!

SO, HENRY IS MY UNCLE. WELL, MY GREAT-UNCLE. AND HE ACCIDENTALLY STARTED A FIRE HERE A LONG TIME AGO.
YOU DON'T SAY.

THAT MOON TOWER HAS MADE A LOT OF PROBLEMS FOR MY FAMILY AND WINDROSE. LIKE MOST THINGS MY UNCLE DID.

CURSED . . .

THE NIGHT OF THE DISASTER, HE THOUGHT HE WAS ON THE PATH TO FIND THE TRUE TREASURE OF WINDROSE.
BUT HE FAILED AND MESSED SO MUCH UP IN THE PROCESS.

MILDRED, WE SHOULD TELL YOU SOMETHING . . .

PLUS ULTRA!

MORE LIKE "NONPLUS ULTRA".

ASHER!
OW!
OW!

HOW DO YOU KNOW HIS DOG'S NAME?
UH . . .

LUCKY GUESS?
MILDRED

WOW, WASN'T THAT GREAT? AND YOU KNOW WHAT TIME IT IS NOW?
WE'RE GOING ON A TREASURE HUNT TO START YOUR SUMMER OFF RIGHT!
Produced by The Windrose Historical Society

YAAA! HOOO! YEAH!!

HERE WE GO AGAIN!
SHHH!
WHAT DO YOU MEAN, AGAIN?

OKAY, FIRST WE HAVE TO--

STOP!
WHAT IS GOING ON?

WHAT DO YOU MEAN?
"LUCKY GUESS," "HERE WE GO AGAIN"? WHAT'S YOUR DEAL? ARE YOU, LIKE . . . SPIES OR SOMETHING?

ACTUALLY, WE PREFER "SECRET AGENTS"!

HOW DO YOU KNOW ALL THOSE THINGS?
WELL, WE . . . WE . . .

CRACK!
WOOOSH!

FLAP!
AHHH!!

COME ON, THIS WAY!

IN HERE!

GOOD TO KNOW THE WEIRD WEATHER HASN'T CHANGED.

OKAY . . .

AS YOU WERE SAYING. . .
MILDRED

THERE'S A LOT TO EXPLAIN.
PRETTY SURE YOU WOULDN'T BELIEVE US IF WE DID.
I WOULDN'T IF I WERE YOU.

YOU'RE RIGHT, AND THEY'RE WRONG ABOUT YOUR FAMILY.
YOU DON'T SAY?
BETH ISN'T KIDDING.

YOUR UNCLES WERE ON THE RIGHT PATH.
HOW DO YOU KNOW THAT?
BECAUSE WE'RE PRETTY SURE THAT WE'RE ON IT NOW.

OKAY, QUIT IT.
THIS ISN'T FUNNY.
MILDRED

WE'RE NOT FROM *CAMP WHATSITCALLED.*
WE'RE FROM CAMP PATHFINDERS.

I'VE NEVER SEEN YOU BEFORE.
YOU WLL IN ABOUT FIFTY YEARS.
58.
WHATEVER.

SO WHAT ARE YOU SAYING?
HAVE YOU EVER NOTICED WEIRD THINGS HAPPEN IN WINDROSE?
BESIDES THE "GRASS GAS."

WELL, YES, OF COURSE. BUT--
MILDRED

WELL, THERE'S A LOT MORE GOING ON THAN THE WEATHER.
YOU HAVE TO BELIEVE US.

WE'RE FROM THE FUTURE!
HARRY!

THIS IS UNBELIEVABLE.
UNBELIEVABLE BUT TRUE.

I KNOW IT SOUNDS CRAZY!
WE STARTED TO DO THE CAMP TREASURE HUNT IN OUR TIME AND SOMEHOW WOUND UP HERE IN 1962.

YOUR UNCLE JACOB TOLD US SOMETHING . . . BUT IN THE FUTURE.

HOW DO I KNOW YOU'RE NOT LYING?

WE HAVE SOMETHING TO SHOW YOU.

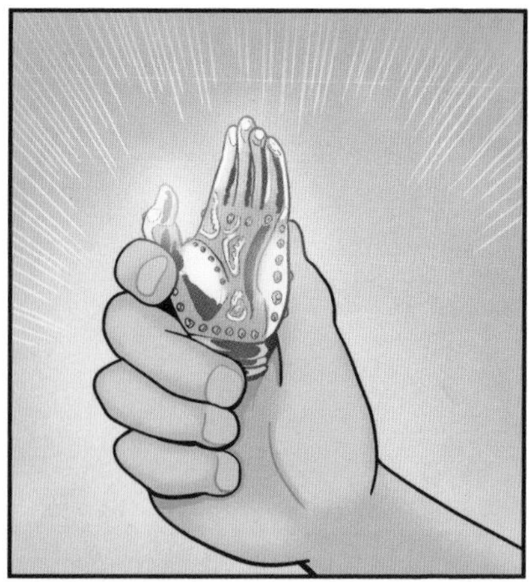

THE BROTHERHOOD!

DOES THAT MEAN YOU BELIEVE US NOW?

MY UNCLE JACOB TOLD ME ABOUT THE HANDS, BUT I NEVER KNEW IF HE WAS JUST TELLING TALL TALES.

HE TOLD ME THAT TIME KIND OF SKIPS AROUND WINDROSE SOMEHOW, BUT I NEVER BELIEVED HIM.
MILDRED

WE THINK SOMETHING HAPPENED HERE THAT MAKES TIME DO WEIRD THINGS.
YOUR UNCLES KNEW THAT.

BUT HENRY DISAPPEARED AFTER THE MOON TOWER ACCIDENT. JACOB LEFT CLUES THAT LED US HERE, AND WE COULD REALLY USE YOUR HELP TO GET BACK HOME.

UH . . . MILDRED, ARE YOU OKAY?

Flint

Henry Merriweather

UH, YOU KNOW WE'RE STILL HERE, RIGHT?

UNCLE JACOB TOLD ME ABOUT A PLACE CALLED RINGING ROCKS. AND HE SAID IT WAS WHERE TIME--
SKIPS?

MAYBE THAT'S WHERE YOU CAN GET HOME?

I THINK IT MIGHT BE!
BUT IT'S REALLY FAR AWAY. I DON'T HAVE ANY IDEA HOW TO GET THERE.

THE CAMP USED TO ATTEMPT EXPEDITIONS THERE, BUT FEW EVER MADE IT ALL THE WAY.
Ringing Rocks
Explorer Badge
(no longer obtainable)

NOW IT'S COMPLETELY OFF-LIMITS.
Flint

THAT'S IT. THAT'S WHERE WE HAVE TO GO.
BUT WE DON'T KNOW HOW TO GET THERE.

HOLD ON . . .
MILDRED

I MIGHT KNOW SOMEONE WHO CAN HELP.

Ringing Rocks or BUST!
I HAVE AN IDEA, BUT IT'S A LONG SHOT.

C'MON, GANG! FOLLOW ME!

THERE'S AN OLD COUNSELOR WHO LIVES HERE.

HE WAS A CAMPER ONCE AND NEVER LEFT. HIS NAME'S GIDEON, AND EVERYONE IS KIND OF SCARED OF HIM, BUT HE'S NICE TO ME.

WHY ARE WE ALWAYS DEALING WITH PEOPLE THAT EVERYONE IS SCARED OF?
HE'S NOT BAD, JUST DIFFERENT. AND HE KNOWS ALL ABOUT THE RIVER LIKE NOBODY ELSE.

GRUMBLE . . .

UM . . . ARE WE SURE HE'S NICE?
MAYBE HE'S JUST NOT A MORNING PERSON.

LET'S GET CLOSER.

OKAY, I'M JUST GOING TO GO SAY HI.

WHAT ARE YOU GOING TO SAY? "HI, IT'S A NICE DAY. MY FRIENDS FROM THE FUTURE NEED YOUR HELP"? DIDN'T YOU SAY HE WAS NICE?

LET'S JUST SAY HE CAN BE MOODY.

OKAY, I GOT THIS. OLD PEOPLE LOVE ME. I VOLUNTEER AT MY MA-MO'S RETIREMENT HOME AND--

GOLLY, NO!
LET ME TALK TO HIM FIRST!

GOOD MORNING, GIDEON!
YUP.

IT'S A PERFECT DAY FOR THE TREASURE HUNT. ARE YOU GOING TO BE HELPING OUT AGAIN THIS YEAR?
YUP.

THIS IS MY FRIEND KYLE.

ARE THOSE KIDS HIDING BACK THERE YOUR FRIENDS, TOO?
UH, YES, THEY ARE.

HELLO, SIR! I LIKE YOUR WALKING STICK. DID YOU CARVE IT YOURSELF?

WHADDAYA KIDS WANT?

A RETURN TICKET TO THE FUTURE?

WE COULD USE YOUR HELP, ACTUALLY. THERE'S A PLACE UPRIVER YOU MAY KNOW ABOUT. THE *RINGING*--

-- *ROCKS.*
WHY? NO ONE GOES THERE ANYMORE.

THAT'S ACTUALLY WHY WE WANT TO GO!
THAT AIN'T A REASON.

EXCUSE ME, GIDEON. CAN WE TALK FOR JUST A MOMENT?

IF YOU'RE GOING TO INTERRUPT MY WORK, YA MAY AS WELL HELP.

SEE, WE NEED TO GET THERE IN ORDER TO COMPLETE A PROJECT FOR SCHOOL.

SCHOOL'S OUT. TRY AGAIN.

IT'S ACTUALLY SOMETHING FOR CAMP PATHFINDER.
IT'S ABOUT MILDRED'S UNCLES!

THE MERRIWEATHER BROTHERS.
I KNOW WHO MILDRED'S UNCLES ARE.

SO, CAN YOU HELP US?

TO GET TO THOSE ROCKS, YOU HAVE TO TRAVERSE THE ROCKLEDGE RIVER. BUT UP WHERE WE'RE TALKING, THAT'S NO RIVER.
IT'S MORE LIKE A SNAKE. MEAN AND IT'S GOT A DEADLY BITE.

BELIEVE ME, WE'RE UP FOR IT. WE'VE BEEN THROUGH A LOT AND--

I'M TOO OLD. YOU'RE TOO YOUNG. THAT TIME HAS PASSED. PLUS NONE OF YOU LOOK LIKE YOU'VE EVER SET FOOT IN A BOAT.
PLEASE, WAIT!

WE'RE REALLY GETTING OUR STEPS IN TODAY!
WE'RE DONE TALKING. NO ONE GOES TO THOSE ROCKS ANYMORE. NOT EVEN ME.

GIDEON, SIR. IT'S IMPORTANT.
THE PATH IS CLOSING.

EVEN IF I WANTED TO HELP, WE'D NEED A ROCKLEDGE RIBBON.

A RIBBON?
SEE, YOU DON'T EVEN KNOW WHAT YOU DON'T KNOW.
PLEASE, GIDEON.

FINE. A RIBBON'S A SPECIAL KIND OF MAP. THEY WERE ROLLED UP AND LONG ENOUGH TO CHART THE LENGTH OF A RIVER. WITHOUT ONE O' THOSE, THAT RIVER'D MAKE SURE YOU NEVER FIND WHAT YOU'RE LOOKING FOR.
IT DOESN'T MATTER. THERE AREN'T ANY RIBBONS LEFT. THAT PLACE IS OFF-LIMITS FOR A GOOD REASON!

IF WE HAD A RIBBON MAP FOR ROCKLEDGE, WOULD YOU HELP US?

I LIKE YOUR SPIRIT! HA HA! SURE, I WOULD HELP YA THEN!

YOU'RE A PATHFINDER, RIGHT, SIR?
ALWAYS HAVE BEEN, ALWAYS WILL BE.

SO, WILL YOU STAKE YOUR VOW ON IT?
AYE. IF YOU HAPPEN T'FIND A MISSIN' 200-YEAR-OLD MAP THEN, SURE, I VOW TO HELP YA'S.

NOW LEAVE ME BE. I HAVE WORK.
THANK YOU. WE'LL BE BACK SOON.

SO, NOW WHAT?
MILDRED

WAIT A MINUTE!

THE HISTORICAL SOCIETY!

OF COURSE!

C'MON!

OH YEAH! IT'S 1962, THE YEAR OF THE RENOVATIONS!
PARDON OUR DUST!
RIGHT! THAT'S WHAT THE MARKER OUTSIDE SAID.

OH GREAT.

·EMPLOYEES ONLY·
DON'T MIND THE MESS.
ALFRED?

ONLY IF I'M IN TROUBLE. YOU CAN CALL ME AL.
WHAT CAN I HELP YOU WITH?

WE ARE LOOKING FOR SOMETHING VERY SPECIFIC AND WONDERED IF YOU COULD HELP US. IT'S FOR A HISTORY PROJECT.

WELL, I DO LOVE A HISTORY MYSTERY. COME ON IN!

WE ARE LOOKING FOR A MAP OF THE ROCKLEDGE RIVER. A RIBBON MAP.

I DON'T BELIEVE I'VE EVER SEEN ONE OF THOSE. BUT YOU'RE WELCOME TO LOOK.

WE RECEIVED A NUMBER OF NAVIGATIONAL TOOLS FROM AN EXPLORER NAMED HENRY--

MERRIWEATHER?
YES, HOW DID YOU KNOW THAT?

HE WAS MY GREAT-UNCLE.
MILDRED

OH MY WORD. THAT IS SOMETHING. HE HAS A LOT OF FANS IN THIS TOWN. AND, WELL . . .

A LOT OF ENEMIES.
THAT DIDN'T STOP ME FROM BECOMING A PATHFINDER!

EXCUSE ME, AL. WHAT ARE THESE?

THIS IS A BRAND-NEW PROJECT WE ARE PUTTING TOGETHER. THE IDEA IS TO TAKE SOME OF OUR ARTIFACTS AND SEAL THEM IN TIME CAPSULES, ALL WITH DIFFERENT CODES TO OPEN THEM.

WE'RE PLANNING ON HIDING THEM THROUGHOUT THE TOWN. IT'S A WAY FOR US TO KEEP OUR HISTORY INTACT AND ALIVE. AND, WELL, FUN.

NEVER SEEN ANYTHING LIKE THIS, RIGHT, HARRY?
Sh!

THIS ROOM MAY BE OF GREAT INTEREST TO YOU.

LOOK!

HARRY STILL HAS THE TIME CAPSULE IN HIS BAG.

NOW, IF YOU LOOK OVER HERE, YOU'LL SEE THERE ARE A NUMBER OF THINGS WE ARE SORTING THROUGH.

HAVE A LOOK THROUGH ALL OF THIS. MAYBE YOU'LL FIND WHAT YOU'RE LOOKING FOR.

I'M JUST DOWN THE HALLWAY IF YOU NEED ANYTHING. AND PLEASE, HANDLE ALL OF THIS WITH CARE.

WOW!

THE TIME CAPSULE!

HOW DID YOU ALREADY GET ONE? IS THIS FROM YOUR CAMP?

YES! OUR COUNSELOR GAVE IT TO US, AND WE THOUGHT IT WAS JUST A PROP OR SOMETHING.

MAYBE IT CONTAINS SOMETHING IMPORTANT.

THERE ARE FOUR SLOTS.
KNOW THY--
Temet Nosce

SELF!

PUT IN "SELF."

CLICK.
SELF!
OF COURSE!

CAN IT BE? A RIBBON?

SHOOF!

THIS IS INCREDIBLE
WE HAD IT ALL ALONG.
MAYBE IT JUST NEEDED TO BE IN THE RIGHT PLACE...
AT THE RIGHT TIME.

I CANNOT BELIEVE THIS.

WELL, LOOKS LIKE GIDEON'S GOING TO HAVE TO KEEP HIS END OF THE BARGAIN.

NEXT STOP--GIDEON!
WINDROSE
HISTORICAL SOCIETY
MUSEUM

GIDEON, WE'RE BACK!
GID-STER, YOU'RE NEVER GONNA GUESS WHAT WE'VE FOUND...

PEOPLE! LOOK HERE!

WHOA . . .
LOOK AT ALL OF THIS.

WOW. GIDEON REALLY CARES ABOUT THIS CAMP.

HEY, LOOK OVER HERE!
1936 Camp Pathfinder

LOOKS LIKE OUR OLD PAL GIDEON WAS A THEATER GEEK.
1st PLACE
Windrose Community Theat
Certificate of Excellence

HE'S ALSO A WRITER.
Act 3
The Way Back

I HAD NO IDEA!

WOW, HE WAS A STRAIGHT-UP ACTOR.

year, community programs are
Castle as enrichment activities
for the Bucks County Historical
have included Winter Wonderland
in the Park, Candlelight Holiday
for Families, Mercer's Night Tales,
Scenes Tours, Escape Rooms, etc.

The Windrose Chronicle
TEN CENTS
TWENTY ONE PAGES
WINDROSE, PA • THURSDAY, MAY 24, 1934
A BLACK-TIE AND BLACKOUT AFFAIR

GIDEON DOES KNOW--

GIDEON DOES KNOW WHAT?
GIDEON! WE FOUND IT!
HOW DID YOU GET IN HERE?
SORRY ABOUT BREAKING IN! WE JUST WANTED TO SHOW YOU--

I . . .

WE HAVE WHAT YOU ASKED FOR.

I'M NOT SURE WHAT YA WANT FROM ME.
CAN YOU HELP GET US TO RINGING ROCKS?

HELP? SURE, I CAN HELP. HERE'S SOME ADVICE: LEAVE THAT MAP BE, AND WHEREVER IT LEADS!

I TOLD YA. THIS AIN'T JUST A RIVER. IT'S DANGEROUS. IT WANTS TO KEEP PEOPLE OUT. LIKE IT'S PROTECTING SOMETHIN'.
THE TREASURE?
THE WAY HOME?
ZOMBIE MERRIWEATHER?!

I WOULD BE HELPING YOU MORE BY KEEPING YOU AWAY.

BUT WE HAVE TO GO. IT'S REALLY IMPORTANT. WE HAVE TO SEE THE RINGING ROCKS.

YOU DON'T GET IT, DO YA? THE ONLY WAY THERE IS UPRIVER, AND BETWEEN THE RAPIDS AND ROCKS . . . EVEN THE BEST PATHFINDERS COULDN'T MAKE IT.
LIKE MY UNCLES?

GREAT MEN, BOTH OF THEM, BUT . . .
DID YA KNOW HENRY?

NO. HE'S BEEN GONE MY WHOLE LIFE.
MILDRED

PLEASE, GIDEON. I NEED TO UNDERSTAND WHAT MY UNCLES WERE TRYING TO FIND.
I THINK THOSE ROCKS HAVE THE ANSWER.

IT'S NOT AN EASY TRIP. WHO'LL BE THE EYES?
WHO'LL BE THE WHAT NOW?

THE EYES! THE PERSON UP FRONT! IN THE CANOES . . . ?

UHHH . . .
MEANING, WHOEVER'S GOT THE KEENEST EYES UP SHOULD BE UP FRONT!

LOOK, ALL RIVERS LEAD SOMEWHERE, BUT THIS ONE GOES TO A PLACE THAT'S--
CURSED?
YOU AND ALL THE CURSING.
LET'S JUST SAY, I LEARNED A LONG TIME AGO, THAT PLACE WANTS TO BE LEFT ALONE.

WE HAVE TO TRY.
YOU SURE YOU'RE UP FOR THIS? ALL OF YOU?

WE DID WHAT YOU ASKED US TO DO. WE VOWED TOGETHER.

YOU DON'T KNOW ANYTHING ABOUT A TRIP LIKE THIS. YOU'D HAFTA TRAIN AS WE GO . . .

WELL, C'MON THEN. TIME'S WASTIN'. WE START NOW!

YES!
AWESOME!
LET'S DO IT!

Chapter
THREE

THERE'S A LOT I WOULD LIKE TO TEACH YA. I'M GONNA SHOW YOU THE FOUR WAYFINDING METHODS.

FIRST THING'S FIRST!
ORIENTATION?

AYE.
ONE OF YA'S WRITE THIS DOWN.

YOU HAVE TO IDENTIFY LANDMARKS ON YER PATH SO YOU DON'T GET LOST. THINGS THAT WON'T CHANGE, TO HELP YOU DETERMINE YOUR LOCATION.

THE NEXT METHOD IS **ROUTE DECISION.** THIS MEANS CHOOSING A DIRECTION TO THE DESTINATION.
I'D CHOOSE THE QUICKEST DIRECTION TO A NAP.
HARRY! SHH!

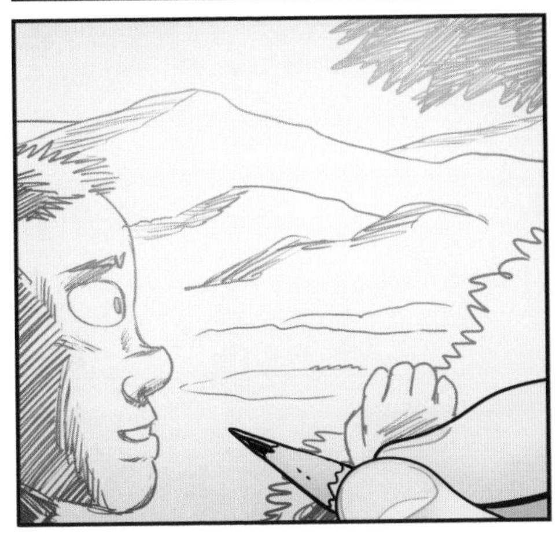

WOW!

STAY FOCUSED ON MARKERS THAT DON'T CHANGE, LIKE MOUNTAINS, TO KEEP YOURSELF GOING IN THE SAME DIRECTION.

TO KNOW WHERE YOU'RE HEADED, YOU NEED A GOAL IN MIND. YOU HAVE TO RECOGNIZE WHEN YOU'VE REACHED YOUR DESTINATION.

KYLE, THIS IS . . .
AMAZING!
THANKS!

TO SUCCEED ON THIS TRIP, YOU HAVE TO WORK TOGETHER. THREE IN EACH. GET IN!

POSITIONS ARE KEY.

TH' MAN UP FRONT IS THE EYES.

THE BACK'S THE TAIL. THEY STEER THE SHIP BY WORKING WITH THE CURRENTS.

BUT THE BELLY BALANCES EVERYTHING.

WHEN THINGS GET ROUGH, THE MIDDLE MAN WILL KEEP YOU UPRIGHT.

HE KNOWS WE'RE NOT ALL MEN, RIGHT?
HE'S AN OLD-TIMER.

COMMUNICATION'S KEY. EYES SEES 'N TELLS THE TAIL. THE BELLY KEEPS THINGS BALANCED.

THAT'S IT. BUT MAKE SURE TO THANK THE WATER 'FORE YA GO.

IS HE SERIOUS?
JUST GO WITH IT.

NOW THE JOURNEY CAN BEGIN.

WHAT'S UP WITH THESE METAL PANELS, GIDEON?

REMEMBER I SAID THE SNAKE HAS A BITE?

WELL, NO POINT IN GOING IF YOU'RE NOT PREPARED. I MADE SOME SPECIAL MODIFICATIONS MYSELF.

I'M WITH YOU, GID. ALWAYS BE READY.

HAVING THE RIGHT TOOL IS HENRY'S THING TOO.

I MISS REGGIE.

SO, WHAT DO YOU KNOW ABOUT THOSE RINGING ROCKS?

VERY LITTLE.
JUST WHAT MY UNCLE TOLD ME.

SO YOU DIDN'T KNOW YOUR UNCLE HENRY?
NO, HE DISAPPEARED BEFORE I WAS BORN.

YOU THINK HE'S--?
NOT DEAD? MY FAMILY DOESN'T THINK SO.

HE WENT MISSING, BUT YOU THINK HE'S STILL ALIVE?

NO ONE REALLY KNOWS.

MY UNCLE JACOB TALKED ABOUT HIM A LOT. AND HE'S THE ONE WHO TOLD ME ABOUT RINGING ROCKS.

AND HE TOLD YOU HOW DANGEROUS THEY ARE?
WELL, I KNOW THAT THEY'RE--

CURSED?
THAT IS ***SO*** NOT HELPFUL.

I JUST DON'T LIKE SCARY THINGS! CURSED THINGS ARE SCARY!

I WAS GOING TO SAY *SPECIAL*. I KNOW THOSE ROCKS ARE CONNECTED TO WHAT MY UNCLE WAS LOOKING FOR THAT NIGHT.

OKAY, HOLD ON.

AAH!
BUMP!
BUMP!
HOLD ON!!

THE BELLY ISN'T BALANCED! MIDDLE SEATS SWITCH!

MIDDLE! SWITCH!

YOU MEAN RIGHT NOW?!

YES, NOW! BEFORE IT GETS WORSE!

UMMMM . . . WE'RE GOOD RIGHT HERE.

YOU'RE NOT! YA HAFTA SWITCH!

MAYBE HARRY SHOULD GO?
WHY ME? I'M NOT GOING TO STAND UP RIGHT NOW!

OKAY! WE'LL SWITCH!

TOO LATE FOR THAT NOW!

UNNNNHHH . . .
NATE, ARE YOU OKAY?

HOLD ON!

AAAAAHH!!

REMEMBER ME!

I CAN'T BELIEVE WE SURVIVED!

MEET AT THAT ISLAND!

ARE YOU OKAY?
YEAH, I THINK SO.

UGH. I'M SOAKED. I DON'T EVEN WANT TO KNOW WHAT MY HAIR LOOKS LIKE.
YOUR HAIR? WHO CARES ABOUT YOUR HAIR?!

COUGH! COUGH!
YOU OKAY?

LOOK AT HER HAIR! SHE'S FINE!
HA HA!

WE ALMOST DIED OUT THERE, AND ALL YOU CARE ABOUT IS YOUR HAIR?
RIDICULOUS!

IT'S NOT ABOUT HAIR, IT'S ABOUT CARE!
BUT YOU'RE TALKING ABOUT HAIR.

YOU JUST DON'T GET IT!

AND ***YOUR*** HAIR LOOKS TERRIBLE!
HA! HA! HA!

HA! HA! HA! HA! HA!
HA! HA!

CHILDREN.
HA! HA! HA! HA! HA! HA! HA! HA! HA! HA! HA! HA!

CHILDREN!

THIS IS ONLY THE BEGINNING. THE RIVER IS NOT GOING TO CARE ABOUT YOUR FIGHTIN'! OR YOUR HAIR! YOU DID NOTHING OUT THERE TO TAKE CARE OF YOURSELVES OR TO WORK AS A TEAM! YOU COULDA DIED!
WE'RE SORRY.

NOW, LET'S GET THE MAP AND UNDERSTAND WHERE WE ARE. I BELIEVE THINGS WILL GET A LOT ROUGHER BEFORE WE LAND AT RINGING ROCKS.

SO, ARE WE HERE?
I DON'T KNOW! MAYBE HERE . . . OR HERE.

THERE ARE METHODS, YOU KNOW. WAYFINDING!
OH RIGHT! LOOK FOR LANDMARKS.

THIS MAP'S REALLY OLD. THE LAND CHANGES.
BUT SOME THINGS CHANGE SLOWER THAN OTHERS.

WHAT'S THAT MEAN?
LOOK FOR THINGS THAT DON'T CHANGE AS MUCH?

LIKE THAT!
OOH, LOOK HERE ON THE RIBBON MAP!

SO WE MUST BE HERE! AND RINGING ROCKS IS UP THERE . . .
THAT MEANS WE HAVE TO STAY TO THE LEFT.
TO SAVE TIME, WE HAVE TO CUT THROUGH ONE OF THOSE NATURAL POOLS.

WHEN WE REACH THIS SYSTEM OF POOLS, WE'LL KNOW WE'RE CLOSE. BUT WE CAN'T RELAX. THE SNAKE IS NOT TO BE TRUSTED! HER CURRENTS ARE SILENT BUT VICIOUS. ONLY ONE POOL WILL LEAD US THROUGH.

THE SNAKE HAS FANGS AND A FORKED TONGUE. WHEN THE TONGUE TOUCHES THE TAIL--
FANGS? THAT DOESN'T SOUND GOOD.
WE'RE NOT GONNA MAKE ANY HEADWAY TODAY. MIGHT AS WELL SET UP CAMP FOR THE NIGHT.

NATE, ARE YOU OKAY?
YEAH, I'M FINE.
I'M REALLY WORRIED ABOUT YOU.
I'M OKAY, REALLY.

LATER.

SO, GIDEON, WHAT IS THE LOST BOY?
WHY YOU ASKIN'?

WE SAW THAT YOU WROTE A STORY OR PLAY ABOUT IT WHEN YOU WERE OUR AGE.
ANY CHANCE YOU STILL REMEMBER IT?

'COURSE I DO!
OH, UH, COOL. I WASN'T TRYING TO SAY YOU'RE OLD . . . I MEAN, I LIKE PLAYS TOO . . . WE HAVE A LOT IN COMMON.

CAN YOU PLEASE TELL US ABOUT IT?
ALRIGHTY, SINCE YA ASKED NICE. TO FOLLOW THIS TALE, YOU HAVE TO GO BACK WHEN THE WORLD WAS YOUNGER AND THERE WERE PATHS PAVED WITH WONDER.

IT WAS A WILD TIME OF ADVENTURE AND DISCOVERY, AND ONE PATHFINDER ROSE ABOVE THE REST. FRANCIS BLARNEY, ALSO KNOWN AS BLARNEY THE BEAR.
HE WAS LARGER-THAN-LIFE 'N KNOWN FAR AND WIDE, FOR HIS TRAVELS BUT ALSO FOR HIS WILD SIDE.

HE'D DO THINGS NO ONE ELSE WOULD, FIND THE WAY WHEN NO ONE ELSE COULD.

USING PATHFINDERS SKILLS WHILE SAILING HIS LEGENDARY *LOST BOY*, HE ACCUMULATED TROVES OF TREASURE, BUT IT WAS NEVER ENOUGH.
UNTIL HE CAUGHT WIND OF WINDROSE AND ITS STREAKS OF SILVER.

THE WINDROSE TREASURE!

AYE. THAT'S WHAT SOME BELIEVE . . . AND WHAT MANY HAVE SEARCHED FOR.

THEY SAY THE *LOST BOY* WAS OUT ON THE SEAS TOO LONG, BECAUSE BLARNEY BECAME OBSESSED WITH THE SILVER.

HE STARTED HAVING VISIONS OF SILVER BUT ALSO FORCES PROTECTING IT.

HE WROTE ABOUT IT ALL IN HIS JOURNALS.

FINALLY, HE MADE IT TO WINDROSE.

HE BELIEVED, LIKE YOUR UNCLES, THERE WAS TREASURE. BUT THAT WAS JUST THE START OF HIS STRUGGLES.

THE *LOST BOY* WAS THE PERFECT TOOL TO PURSUE THE PATH, BUT BLARNEY PUSHED THAT PROUD SHIP TO ITS LIMITS.

BLARNEY WOULDN'T GIVE UP AND HE BECAME MORE AND MORE MAD.

AND FOR THE FIRST TIME, BLARNEY WAS LOST.

THAT IS THE END OF THE BLARNEY LEGEND.

THAT'S IT?!
WHAT HAPPENED NEXT?

NO ONE KNOWS. BLARNEY STOPPED HIS FEVERISH WRITIN' WHEN THEY GOT TO THOSE ROCKS.

DID THEY FIND THE TREASURE?
DID THEY ALL DIE?
MAYBE. THE ANSWERS HAVE ALL BEEN LOST TO TIME.

WHEN I WAS A BOY, I KNEW YOUR UNCLE WELL. HE BELIEVED BLARNEY PAVED THE WAY.

BUT NO ONE ELSE DID.

AFTER THE MOONTOWER AND HIS BROTHER'S BETRAYAL, HENRY LEFT WINDROSE.

BUT I COULDN'T LET IT GO.

I BELIEVED.

BUT THOSE WATERS HAD OTHER IDEAS.

YOUR UNCLE JACOB SAVED ME.

HE FOUND ONE LOST BOY, BUT NEVER FOUND THAT SHIP.

NO ONE EVER HEARD FROM HENRY AGAIN.

SO, IF WE FIND THE SHIP, ARE WE GOING TO FINALLY FIND THE TREASURE OF WINDROSE?
AH, THAT. COUNTLESS TREASURE HUNTERS CAME UP EMPTY HANDED. SEEMS THEY WERE ALWAYS MISSING IT.

LOOK AROUND YOU. THERE'S TREASURE EVERYWHERE, ISN'T THERE?

DON'T THINK BLARNEY EVER GOT THAT.

STORYTIME'S OVER. GET YER REST. TOMORROW, WE FACE THE SNAKE.

THE NEXT MORNING.

IS IT JUST ME OR ARE WE FINALLY GETTING THE HANG OF THIS?

DON'T GET TOO COMFORTABLE.

WHOA!

CAREFUL OF THE FANGS!
YA THINK?!

SSCRAPE...

SEE, PREPARATION WAS KEY.
A.B.R.! ALWAYS BE READY!

THE FORKED TONGUE!

EVERYONE TO THE LEFT!

WORKIN' ON IT!

REMEMBER US!

KEEP LEFT!
I'LL GET THEM.

OKAY, I'M HERE. RELAX.

THAT'S IT. LOOK AROUND,
SEE THE CURRENTS.
DON'T FIGHT THEM.

I SEE IT.

GOOD. WHERE ARE THEY LEADING?
LEFT, THEN RIGHT.

OKAY, TAIL, YOU HEARD HIM! WHEN I SAY, PADDLE OPPOSITE-- RIGHT THEN LEFT.
RIGHT THEN LEFT, WHEN YOU SAY. GOT IT!

NOW WHEN I SAY, YOU ALL PADDLE AS ONE!

PADDLE RIGHT! NOW LEFT!

THAT'S IT!

WHOA!
BUMP!
GIDEON!

I'LL BE OKAY! KEEP GOING!

SHOULD WE GO BACK?
HE'LL BE ALRIGHT. WE HAVE TO KEEP GOING.

Sniff!
OH WOW. SOMETHING SMELLS DIFFERENT.

HER NOSE KNOWS!

LATER.
I THINK THIS IS THAT POOL AREA FROM THE MAP, WE'RE CLOSE!
BUT WHICH WAY DO WE TAKE?

GIDEON ALSO SAID, "WHEN THE TONGUE TOUCHES THE TAIL."

LOOK, THAT ONE SEEMS TO CUT THROUGH TO THE OTHER SIDE!

BETH, CHECK THE MAP.
RIGHT.

TONGUE AND TAIL? LET ME SEE.

THIS IS
WHERE WE
NEED TO LAND.

I THINK IT'S TIME.
TIME FOR WHAT?

IS EVERYTHING OKAY?
YES, EVERYTHING'S FINE.

NATE!
UH!

WHAT . . . HAPPENED?

I'M JUST SO TIRED.
LET'S SET UP CAMP SO YOU CAN GET SOME REST.

Z...

SHOW'S OVER. HE'S ALREADY ASLEEP.

MILDRED, CAN YOU MAKE A FIRE?
MILDRED

DOES A BEAR SLEEP IN THE WOODS?
I THINK THAT'S A *YES.*

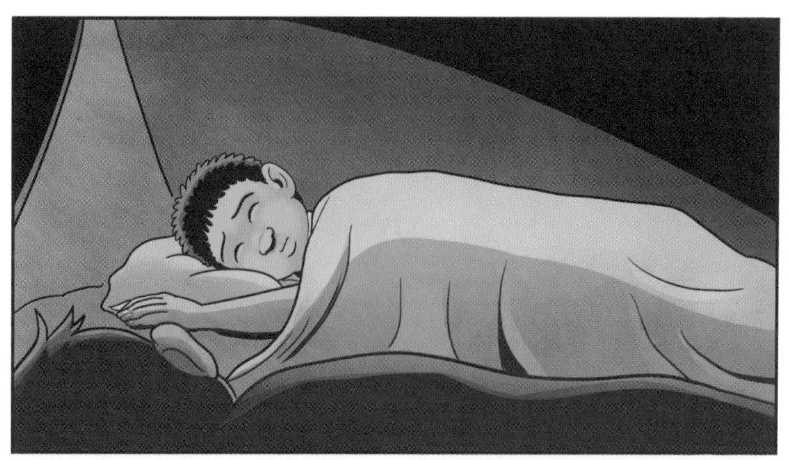

BOOWOONCH!!

BOOWOONCH!

Chapter
FOUR

BOOWOONCH!!

HOW LONG HAVE WE BEEN ASLEEP?
I DON'T KNOW, BUT I FEEL GREAT.

WHAT WAS THAT SOUND?

SOMEONE CHECK ON NATE.

NATE'S GONE!
HE'S WHAT?!

LET'S NOT PANIC.
WHY SHOULD WE NOT PANIC?
WHAT IS GOING ON WITH YOU TWO?

NATE TOLD ME HE HAD TO DO SOMETHING.
WHAT KIND OF SOMETHING?
I DON'T KNOW.

HE SAID THAT THE PATH WAS CLOSING AND THAT SOMETHING WAS SUPPOSED TO HAPPEN.

WHY DIDN'T YOU TELL US?!
HE MADE ME VOW NOT TO SAY ANYTHING.

WHY DID HE TELL ***YOU*** AND NOT ***ME?***
THAT'S WHAT YOU'RE HUNG UP ABOUT RIGHT NOW?

HE COULD BE IN DANGER!

HE ASKED ME TO TRUST HIM, AND I KNOW THAT'S WHAT HE WANTS US ALL TO--

BOOWOONCH!

BOOOWAAUCH!
WHAAT'S GOING-G-G ONNNN?

WELL, THAT WAS UNUSUAL.
I READ ABOUT THIS! THIS WHOLE AREA USED TO BE UNDERWATER. BUT THAT WAS A LONG TIME AGO.

WAS THAT A TIME-HOP?
IF IT WAS, THEY'RE GETTING WORSE!
MILDRED

LOOK! ASHER'S PAWPRINTS!

LET'S FOLLOW THEM!
WE'RE COMING, NATE!

BOOOMWAUNCH!
NAAATE!
THHHAAAAT WAAAAY. WE HAVE TO FOLLOW THE TRACKS!

WOOOSH!

WE FOUND THE *LOST BOY*.
ONE BOY FOUND, ONE TO GO!

I'D RECOGNIZE THOSE SIZE 7'S ANYWHERE. COME ON!

THE RINGING ROCKS!
WE MADE IT!
EVERYONE GRAB HANDS!
PLUS ULTRA!

NOW WHAT?
HOW DO WE KNOW WHAT TO DO NOW?
MAYBE WE SHOULD CHECK THE RIBBON MAP.
DO YOU SEE THIS WRITING? IT'S CUT OFF, LIKE IT'S NOT FINISHED.
SAME ON THIS SIDE.

WHAT IF YOU CONNECT ONE END WITH THE OTHER?
TONGUE AND TAIL! THE CLUE WAS ABOUT THE RIBBON!

The rocks that ring make the symphony sing.
Find the key's tone and you are halfway home.

LOOK!

THAT MUST BE THE KEYSTONE.

YES. FIND DECENT SIZE ROCKS TO RING WITH.
LET'S START A ROCK BAND!

ANY LUCK SO FAR?
BANG!

NOT . . .
DINK.
YET.

"FIND THE KEY'S TONE AND YOU ARE HALFWAY HOME."
KEEP YOUR EYES PEELED FOR ONE OF THOSE!

CRAASH!
EEWOOOONN...
WE BETTER FIGURE THIS OUT QUICK. I'M NOT SURE WE'RE WELCOME HERE MUCH LONGER.

ANYONE WANNA GUESS HOW MANY ROCKS ARE IN THIS FIELD?

SURE, BUT ANOTHER TIME?! LET'S GET RINGING!

BANG!
BONK!
DINK!
BANG!
DONK!

BRRRSSSH!

DINK!
DONK!
DING!

HEY! I THINK I FOUND ONE!

I HEARD IT. STAY THERE, KYLE. ONE OF US HAS TO FIND A KEYSTONE!

YES, I FOUND ANOTHER, BUT NOT THE KEYSTONE YET!
OOOO...

DING!
DING!
DING!
SOMETHING'S HAPPENING!

GOT ANOTHER!
DING!

HARRY! WE NEED YOU TO FIND YOURS!
DINK.
DONK.

DINK!
I'M NOT...
DONK.

DUNK-
FINDING IT!
DONK-

RUMBLE...
CRACK!

DON'T STOP. WE NEED TO COMPLETE THE SYMPHONY.
BANG!
DONK.

WHOA!
WOOOSH!

I'M TRYING!
IT'S KINDA HARD TO CONCENTRATE WITH A WIND MONSTER FLYING AROUND MY HEAD!

COME ON! I NEED TO FIND A ROCK WITH A--

OH . . . LOOK AT YOU!

HURRY!
DING!

LOOK OUT!

WOOOSH!

OWW!
MILDRED!

I CAN'T SEE!

WONG!
SOMETHING IS TRYING TO STOP US!
WONG!

UH, HARRY?

AHHH!
KYLE!

THAT THING IS COMING BACK!

WE HAVE ONE MORE CHANCE! COME ON, HARRY!

DONK!

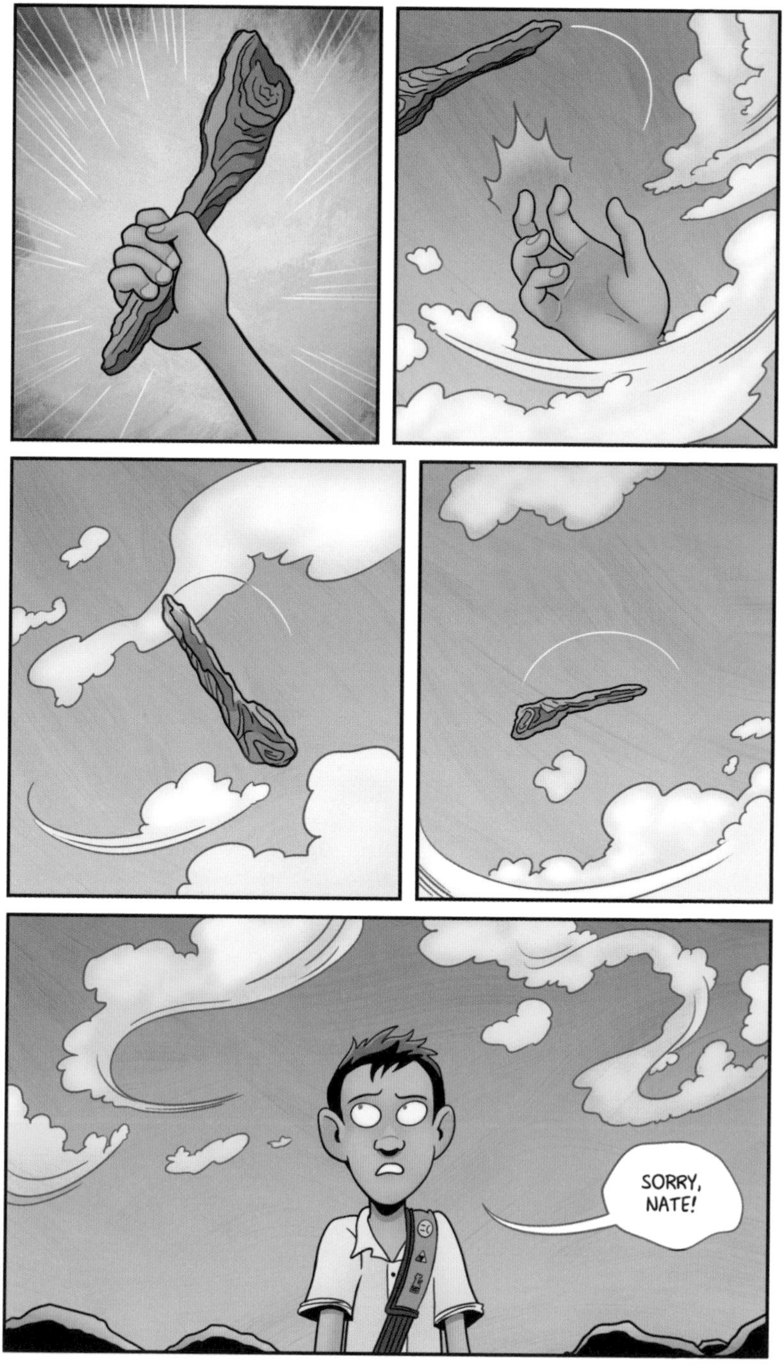

SORRY,
NATE!

OH NO YOU DON'T!
CLUTCH!

A . . . B . . . R!
GIDEON! YOU'RE SAFE!

I GOT YOU. NOW GO DO WHAT YOU CAME TO DO.

YOU HEARD HIM. LET'S FIND A PATH, PATHFINDERS.

DING!
BONG!
BONG!
BWONG!

IT'S WORKING!

SCREEEEE!
WATCH OUT!

FOOOM!

REMMMMMEMBER MEEEEE!
THAT'S NATE! WE HAVE TO GO IN!

LIKE, IN THERE?
YES! WE HAVE TO HELP HIM!

HE WOULD DO IT FOR US!

SPLASH!

WAIT FOR US!
TOGETHER!

YOU BETTER GET GOING. YOUR FRIENDS NEED YA.
READY?
NOT REALLY.

WHAT ARE YOU FEELING?
I FEEL LOST.

SOUNDS ABOUT RIGHT. YOU CAN OFTEN FEEL LOST WHEN YER PATH LEADS TO NEW PLACES.

HOW DID WE GET HERE? WHERE ARE WE GOING?

A BETTER QUESTION IS-- WHAT'S SOMETHIN' YOU KNOW RIGHT NOW?
WE KNOW THAT OUR FRIENDS NEED US.
YEAH . . .

SO WHAT ARE YOU GONNA DO WITH THAT KNOWIN'?

LET'S DO THIS FOR NATE.

FOR OUR FRIENDS!

I'LL KEEP THE PORTAL OPEN. YOU GO HELP YER FRIENDS.
PLUS ULTRA!

COUGH,
COUGH!

KYLE! YOU MADE IT!
VIC!
HARRY!

WHERE ARE WE?
WE'RE STILL FIGURING THAT OUT.

THANKS FOR DROPPING IN!

NATE!
YOU REMEMBERED ME!

YOU HAD US WORRIED!
AW MAN, IT'S GOOD TO SEE YOU.

ARE YOU OKAY?
YEAH. SORRY ABOUT LEAVING. IT WAS IMPORTANT.

INTERESTING . . .
IS THAT CAPTAIN BLARNEY?!

NOT QUITE.
UNCLE . . .
MILDRED

. . . HENRY?!

SO COOL, RIGHT?
. . .
MILDRED

THAT'S AMAZING. WHAT'S HE DOING?

WE'RE NOT COMPLETELY SURE.
SOME INTENSE CALCULATIONS--THAT'S WHY HE'S OUT HERE.

WHICH LEADS TO MY NEXT MAJOR QUESTION . . . WHERE IS HERE?

WELL, THERE'S GOOD NEWS AND THERE'S BAD NEWS.

SO, WHY HASN'T UNCLE HENRY AGED?

AS FAR AS I CAN GATHER, OUT HERE THERE'S NO TIME. BUT DOWN THERE . . .

YES. IT'S LIKE ALL TIMES ARE HAPPENING AT ONCE. BUT--

THERE ARE CREATURES OUT THERE THAT GUARD THESE WATERS. THE SHIP IS SAFE WHERE IT IS, BUT IF IT MOVES, THOSE THINGS WILL CRUSH US.
THAT'S THE BAD NEWS.

UH, GREAT.

AS FAR AS I CAN TELL, HENRY DOESN'T CARE. HE'S HAPPY TO WATCH IT ALL FLOAT BY AND OBSERVE.

OKAY, I MAY BE THE NEW KID, BUT THIS ISN'T THE HENRY MERRIWEATHER I WAS EXPECTING.
I THINK WE'RE PAST "NEW KID" LABELS, BUT I AGREE COMPLETELY WITH YOUR OTHER POINT. WHO IS THIS GUY?

INTERESTING.
UH, MR. MERRIWEATHER?

HMM? OH YES, OF COURSE. I'M VERY BUSY. YOU'LL JUST HAVE TO FOLLOW!
VERY BUSY?

MY APOLOGIES.
I'VE LEARNED TO OBSERVE SO MANY TIMELINES AT ONCE THAT I SOMETIMES FORGET WHAT'S HAPPENING IN THE NOW.
THINGS CAN GET A LITTLE DISTORTED OUT HERE.

HOW LONG HAVE YOU BEEN IN THIS PLACE?
BARK! BARK!

ASHER!
I CAN'T BELIEVE IT.

YES, THAT IS ASHER, BUT IT SEEMS YOU ALREADY KNOW THAT.
I
II
III
IV
V
VI
VII

I DON'T KNOW HOW LONG WE HAVE BEEN HERE. IT IS QUITE AN ACCOMPLISHMENT THAT YOU'VE MADE IT THIS FAR.
Northern Lights

I WAS CURIOUS IF YOUR ARRIVAL WOULD INFLUENCE THINGS, BUT THE PATH IS STILL CLOSING AND TIME IS INDEED RUNNING OUT . . . FASCINATING.
MILDRED

SO IT'S TRUE . . .
YOU'RE MY--
THAT'S
RIGHT . . .

I'M YOUR
UNCLE HENRY.

YOU'VE GROWN
UP TO BECOME
QUITE CLEVER.
THANKS,
I GUESS.

UH, MR. MERRI . . .
WHERE ARE WE?
WE'RE ON
THE *LOST BOY*.

WE THOUGHT THE
LOST BOY WENT
MISSING.
CLICK.

THIS IS MY VERSION
OF THE *LOST BOY*,
THE PERFECT TOOL
TO PURSUE
THE PATH.

WHERE ARE YOU HEADED?
NOWHERE.

SO, YOU MEAN . . .
YOU WANT TO BE ON THIS SHIP?
STUCK IN TIME?

"STUCK"? FAR FROM IT. I'VE FOUND AN ANCHOR OUTSIDE OF THE ENDLESS PARADE, AND NOW I HAVE ALL THE TIME IN THE WORLD TO ENJOY THE SHOW.
BARK!

SORRY, ASHER, WE HAVE ALL THE TIME IN THE WORLD.

WHAT ABOUT MORE BEYOND?

NO NEED FOR MORE WHEN YOU'VE ARRIVED.

I WAS GOING TO SHOW THEM AT THE MOONTOWER . . .

THESE STREAMS, THESE PORTALS . . . THESE NATURAL WONDERS ALL AROUND WINDROSE AND OTHER PLACES ARE CONNECTED AND NEED TO BE PROTECTED.

BUT MY BROTHER FORFEITED HIS VOW, AND IT ALL WENT HORRIBLY WRONG.

WAIT, HOLD ON! JACOB DIDN'T--WELL, YES, HE DID FORFEIT THE VOW.
BUT THEN HE DIDN'T.
AFTER YOU LEFT, HE CHANGED!
HE'S THE REASON WE'RE HERE.

HE BELIEVED IN THE PATH, IN THE BROTHERHOOD.
BUT HE WAS TOO OLD TO CONTINUE ON, SO HE LEFT A TRAIL FOR SOMEONE--

US!
WE DID PRETTY WELL FOLLOWING THE BREAD CRUMBS, I MUST SAY.

HE WANTED TO HEAL THE FRACTURE AND CREATE A NEW PATH, SO NOW WE NEED YOUR HELP.
I CAN'T BELIEVE I'M ASKING MY DEAD UNCLE FOR HELP!

PARDON ME, DO I LOOK DEAD?

MR. MERRIWEATHER, WINDROSE IS IN TROUBLE. WE NEED TO GO BACK AND HELP HEAL IT.
THE PATH CLOSES DURING THE FULL MOON IN YOUR TIME, BUT WE'RE STUCK IN THIS CURRENT. EVEN IF WE BREAK FREE, THERE ARE SERPENTS OUT THERE.

WE'VE DEALT WITH CREEPERS, SNAKE RIVERS, ROCK SPIRITS . . . HOW BAD CAN TIME-SERPENTS BE?

IF WE DON'T GO BACK AND HELP, THE TREASURE COULD BE LOST FOREVER.
WE NEED YOU. WINDROSE NEEDS YOU.
YOU MUST FINISH WHAT I STARTED. THE TOWER IS THE KEY, BUT I'VE BEEN HERE SO LONG, I CAN'T REMEMBER WHY. GO BACK TO THE NIGHT OF THE DISASTER. I CAN LEAD YOU THERE.

SO YOU'LL HELP US? WHAT DO YOU SAY?

I SAY ***PLUS ULTRA!***
PLUS ULTRA!

SO WE'RE STUCK HERE, BUT WE JUST NEED A WAY TO GET UNSTUCK . . .
SOMETHING TO GET US OUT OF THIS GROOVE AND BACK ON TRACK.

WAIT A MINUTE!
I HAVE AN IDEA . . .

CLATCH!

WHEN WE GET THE SIGNAL, YOU BOTH PULL THESE ROPES HARD AND FAST.

GOT IT!
BUT NOT FOR LONG!
READY FOR MY
COMMAND?

HOLD!
THAT'S IT,
GO!

HOIST!
PULL!

THAT'S IT, CREW! WORK TOGETHER!

A LITTLE MORE!
OOSH!

I THINK I GOT IT!

RELEASE THE HOOK!

THAT'S IT, WE DID IT!

THE CURRENTS ARE TOO STRONG HERE. YOU HAVE TO GO NOW.

BUT YOU'LL BE PULLED BACK. I THOUGHT YOU WERE READY TO BE FREE AND EXPLORE MORE.
THE MOST IMPORTANT THING IS FOR YOU TO FINISH YOUR MISSION AND HELP WINDROSE.

I WANT TO THANK YOU ALL.
FOR WHAT?

I FEEL LIKE I WAS BLIND, BUT NOW I CAN SEE. I WAS LOOKING OUT SO FAR, AND YOU REMINDED ME OF WHAT'S IMPORTANT RIGHT IN FRONT OF ME.

WE NEED TO GET YOU ON YOUR WAY. BUT BEFORE YOU GO, TAKE THIS.

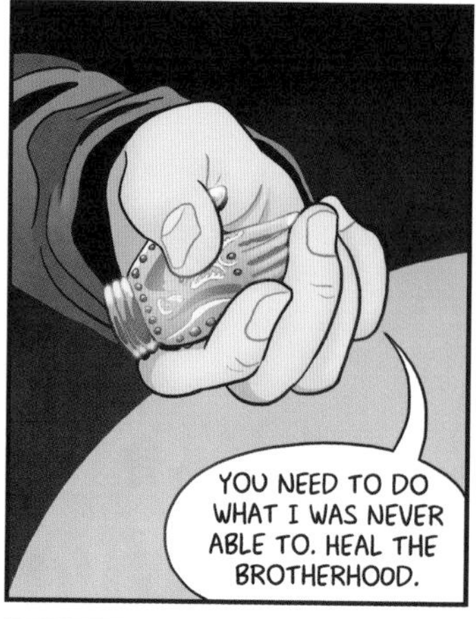
YOU NEED TO DO WHAT I WAS NEVER ABLE TO. HEAL THE BROTHERHOOD.

THANK YOU, WE WILL.

AND, MILDRED, THIS IS FOR YOU.

IT WAS MY GRANDMOTHER'S. SHE WAS POWERFUL AND TALENTED AND A LOT LIKE YOU. I WOULD LIKE YOU TO STAY WITH ASHER AND ME A LITTLE LONGER, THERE IS SOMETHING IMPORTANT I COULD USE YOUR HELP WITH.

THE REST OF YOU . . .

GO HELP CHART A BETTER PATH FOR WINDROSE.

Chapter
FIVE

LET'S GET BEHIND THAT LEDGE.

WE NEED TO STOP THIS PERFORMANCE IMMEDIATELY.
PERFORMANCE?

I'M TELLING YOU, BROTHER, THIS ISN'T THE WAY. WE HAVE NO IDEA WHAT THIS COULD LEAD TO. THIS COULD BE DANGEROUS!

IT WILL BE DANGEROUS NOT TO ACT. YOU HAVE THAT RAT, FAIRLY, SQUEAKING IN YOUR EAR. WE MUST CHANGE OUR WAYS. IF WE DON'T IT WILL BE TEN TIMES WORSE LATER. THE FAIL-SAFE, IT'S THE ONLY WAY TO PROTECT WINDROSE.

YOU THINK HE MEANS FAIRLY? FROM THE GOON PLATOON AT CAMP
AND WE KNOW ONE TOO.
THEY'RE DEFINITELY NOT THE NICEST FAMILY.

WE CANNOT KEEP GOING IN THESE CIRCLES. THOSE CHILDHOOD DREAMS ARE OVER. WINDROSE DOESN'T NEED PROTECTION. IT NEEDS MONEY, OR ELSE IT'S GOING TO FADE AWAY.

DON'T BE LIKE THE REST OF THEM. REMEMBER OUR VOW. THE PATH IS REAL.

I NEED YOU TO GIVE ME THE HAND. WE MUST COMPLETE THIS. TONIGHT!
I WON'T DO IT.

YOU KNOW AS WELL AS I DO, THIS IS THE TIME. THIS MOMENT WILL NOT RETURN FOR--

ONE HUNDRED YEARS?

THAT WAS MERELY A GAME. BROTHER, IT'S TIME TO MOVE ON. IT WON'T MAKE A DIFFERENCE IF YOU HAVE MY HAND OR NOT.

HENRY, EVERYONE IS WAITING. ARE YOU READY?

ARE YOU ALRIGHT?
I . . . I DON'T KNOW.

SHOULD WE DO SOMETHING?
NO, I DON'T THINK THAT'S A GOOD IDEA.
JUST TAKE NOTES.
ON IT!

I DON'T KNOW IF THIS WILL WORK. BUT THE SHOW MUST GO ON.

AS MANY OF YOU KNOW, I'VE LONG BEEN SEARCHING FOR PROOF OF THE FABLED WINDROSE TREASURE. TONIGHT I WILL LIGHT THE WAY. ON THE NIGHT OF THIS LEGENDARY SUPER MOON, THE PATH WILL BE REVEALED.

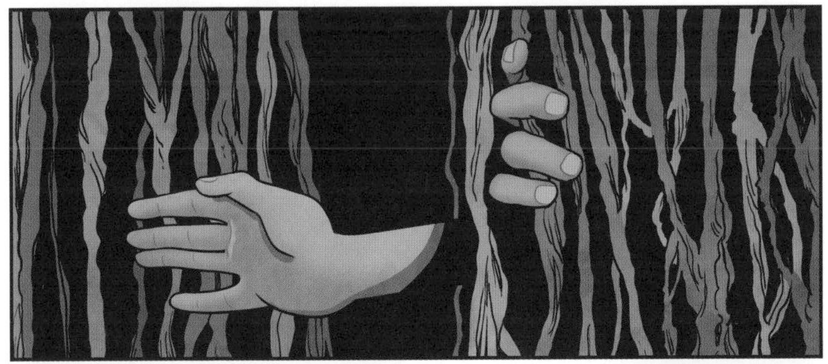

WHOA, HAVE WE BEEN HERE BEFORE?

CRACK!
RUMBLE...

ALL HE NEEDED TO DO WAS GIVE HENRY THE HAND.
RUMBLE
THE HANDS NEEDED TO BE IN THE MOSAIC.

IS THIS IT? IS THIS THE EXACT RIGHT TIME?!

YES, LOOK!

YAAA! HOOO!
YEAH!!

COME ON, THERE'S NOT MUCH TIME!
THE BROTHERHOOD!

EVERYONE, START LOOKING FOR THE MOSAIC!
THERE! I THINK I SEE IT!

COME ON!

WATCH OUT! THE GROUND IS MOVING!

IS IT AN EARTHQUAKE?

RUMBLE...

CRACK!

RUMBLE...

SAVING THE WEIRDEST WEATHER FOR THE LAST, I GUESS.

CRACK!
BOOM!

SCATTER!
RUMBLE...
CRACK!

CRACK-PSHH!

THAT'S THE WATER FROM THE LABYRINTH!

HURRY! WE HAVE TO CONNECT THE HANDS!
I FOUND THE MOSAIC!
CRACK...
RUMBLE...

THIS MUST BE WHERE THE HANDS FIT INTO!
NATE, IS THE MOON STONE READY?

GOT IT!

"WITH THIS STONE, I PRESENT TO YOU WHAT I BELIEVE COULD BE THE MOST VALUABLE VIEW EVER SEEN. THE PATH FORWARD."

I HOPE I CAN DO THIS THE WAY MERRI DID WAY BACK WHEN.
HERE WE GO.

I HAVE THE HOLDER.
LET'S DO THIS. *PLUS ULTRA!*

WE'RE DOING THIS FOR YOU, MILDRED!

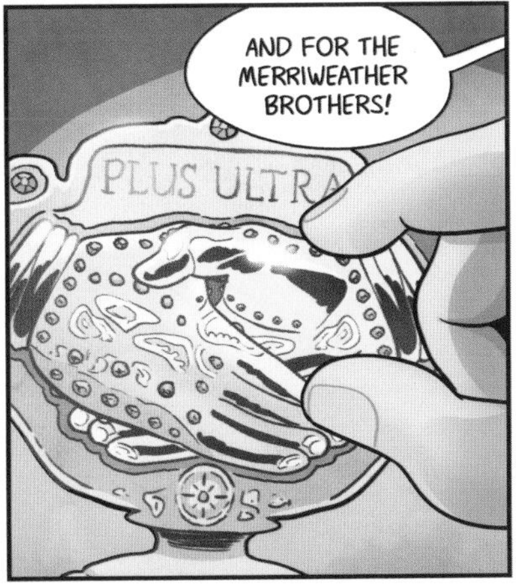
AND FOR THE MERRIWEATHER BROTHERS!
PLUS ULTRA

CLICK.
PLUS ULTRA

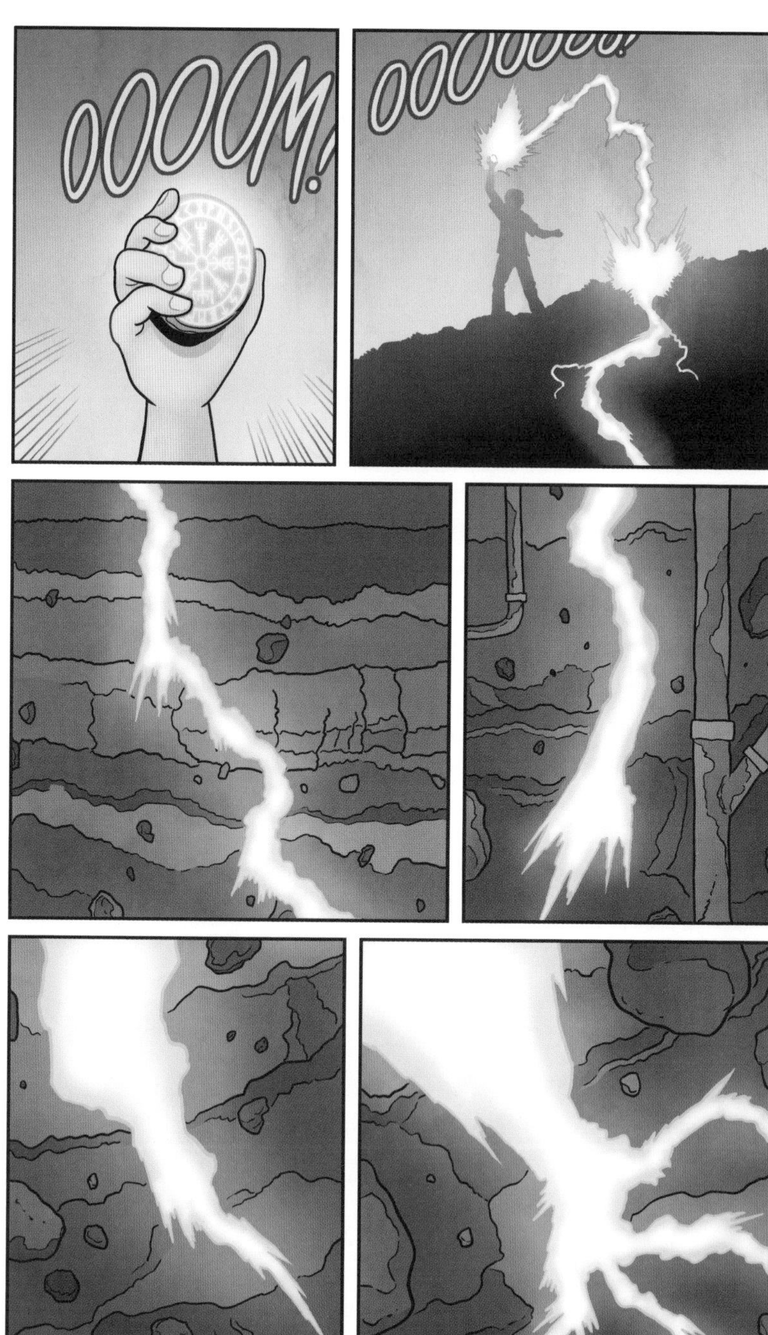
OOOOM!
OOOOOOOO!

OOOOO-SH-KRACK!

COOM!
CRACK!
IT'S BEING DESTROYED FROM THE INSIDE OUT!
SHRACK!

CRACK!

DWOOOONG!

DWOOOOOWING!
NO TURN ON RED
P

CRINK!
TINK!
TINK...
CRACK.
CRACK!
TINK
TINK

WHOA!

POP!
POP!
POP!
POP!
POP!

WAIT . . . IS THIS . . .
THE TREASURE?

WINDROSE!

C'MON!

WE HAVE TO FIND MILDRED!
MAIN ST

THERE SHE IS!

MILDRED!
HELLO, OLD FRIENDS!

DID YOU KNOW ALL ALONG?

NOT ALL ALONG. I HAD FORGOTTEN MANY THINGS OVER THE YEARS. FORGOTTEN THAT IT'S OKAY TO BELIEVE IN MAGIC.

POOF!

EXACTLY!
HA! HA! HA! HA! HA! HA! HA!

WHOA . . .

AND LOOK!

SILVER?!

THE LEGEND IS REAL!

SILVER!

I THINK WE FINALLY FOUND THE TREASURE.
IT LOOKS LIKE EVERYONE DID.

Windrose Moon Festival

WOW! DID WE . . .
I THINK WE SET THINGS RIGHT.
WAIT! DO YOU SMELL THAT TOO?

IT WASN'T ME!

OW!
SHOVE.

THE WIND SMELLS LIKE ROSES!

LOOK!

IT LOOKS LIKE MERRIWEATHER FINALLY GOT FREE.
READY TO EXPLORE FURTHER BEYOND!

HARRY, NATE, VIC, BETH, AND KYLE . . . YOU ARE THE TRUE PATHFINDERS, GUARDIANS OF WINDROSE.

YOU HAVE CONTINUED ON WHERE MY GREAT-UNCLES LED, AND FORGED YOUR OWN WAY FORWARD. TODAY IS A GRAND DAY AND NOW YOU ARE READY FOR ADVENTURES AHEAD.

The End